愛閱雙語叢書適讀對象：
具國中以上英文閱讀能力者

The Land of the Immortals

仙人之谷

Jonathan Augustine　著

Machi Takagi　繪

三民書局

國家圖書館出版品預行編目資料

The Land of the Immortals:仙人之谷 / Jonathan Augustine
著;Machi Takagi繪;本局編輯部譯.－－初版一刷.－－
臺北市：三民，2005
　　面；　　公分.－－(愛閱雙語叢書.世界故事集系列)
中英對照
ISBN 957－14－4232－1　 (平裝)

　1.英國語言－讀本

805.18　　　　　　　　　　　　　　94001421

網路書店位址　http://www.sanmin.com.tw

© The Land of the Immortals

—— 仙人之谷

著作人　Jonathan Augustine
繪　者　Machi Takagi
譯　者　本局編輯部
發行人　劉振強
著作財
產權人　三民書局股份有限公司
　　　　臺北市復興北路386號
發行所　三民書局股份有限公司
　　　　地址／臺北市復興北路386號
　　　　電話／(02)25006600
　　　　郵撥／0009998－5
印刷所　三民書局股份有限公司
門市部　復北店／臺北市復興北路386號
　　　　重南店／臺北市重慶南路一段61號
初版一刷　2005年2月
編　號　S 805160
定　價　新臺幣貳佰參拾元整
行政院新聞局登記證局版臺業字第○二○○號

ISBN　957－14－4232－1　　(平裝)

TO OUR BELOVED DAUGHTERS
MAYU AND YUMI

In a house full of servants in the capital of China lived a wealthy noble family. Every autumn, when the local pastry shops baked their traditional moon cakes, the master of the family invited local scholars and officials to a big banquet. This year for the first time the master's son, Fei-long, was allowed to join the party. From his corner of the table, Fei-long watched the important men sip their wine, and admired the plumes of smoke that floated from their pipes.

As the full moon peered into the living room, the oldest scholar of the group tapped the marble floor with his lacquered cane for everyone's attention. Then pointing west, he whispered, "In the edge of this empire is a mountain range with lofty peaks that soar high above the clouds. The Zhen mountains have been the home of the immortals since heaven and earth were separated. When I was young I stumbled along these mountains' winding paths and eventually came across a temple, built out over the edge of a fearsome cliff. I never entered this temple, but I heard that the monks there can leap barefoot over the treetops and mountain peaks."

The cheeks of the scholars turned as red as their silk robes while they sipped their wine half asleep. But Fei-long listened attentively, so the old gentleman drew him a map of the Zhen mountains. When the guests finally staggered to their feet to thank the master, hardly anyone knew where they were or what had been said.

紅沙漠

For the next few weeks Fei-long could not get the Zhen mountains out of his mind. He would show his father the map and beg for his permission to make the journey, but his father's answer was always, "No!"

"Absolutely not!" he roared one morning, when Fei-long had interrupted him in the middle of an important meeting at the Emperor's court. "Enter the monastery of the Zhen mountains? I didn't spend all these years raising a son to become a monk!" he shouted. But finally seeing that Fei-long would not stop pestering him, he finally gave his blessings.

The next day Fei-long started off with two horses carrying his belongings. After several days the mountain trail became so treacherous that he had to leave everything behind, including the horses. Just when he was beginning to think that he had been fooled, Fei-long found the cave that the old gentleman had drawn on the map. He lit his candle, got down on his knees and crawled through the narrow cave. As he approached the light at the other end of the narrow passage, he could make out a small temple on the edge of a cliff.

When Fei-long reached the temple, he found an old man with a long white beard sitting silently on a mat. Fei-long could not guess the age of this strange character, since his wild eyes reminded Fei-long of the mischievous kids that roamed the streets of his hometown. But when the old man greeted him in a deep calm voice, Fei-long suddenly felt as if he could endure anything. Summoning up his courage, Fei-long asked whether he could study the mysterious ways of the immortals under his supervision. The old master looked straight into Fei-long's eyes and said, "I am afraid that you won't be able to bear the training."

"No matter what, I promise I won't give up," insisted Fei-long.

"Remember those words," said the old master as he disappeared into the temple.

The next day ten disciples gathered in the central hall and gave Fei-long a coarse cotton robe. After Fei-long got dressed, he watched them scoop a handful of water and brush their teeth with their fingers without even wasting a drop of water.

Then he was given an ax and was told to go into the mountains to gather firewood.

When he returned with a huge bundle of wood, his next job was chopping vegetables.

Finally after dinner when he felt he had to take a rest, he was ordered to chop wood for the bath.

Fei-long worked diligently for the next few months. Calluses covered his hands and his robes turned into rags. Each day he expected his work to get easier, but as the days grew shorter his hopes were buried in the snow. But since none of the other disciples complained, he continued to look for firewood every day.

One cold winter afternoon, Fei-long could no longer bear his training and decided to go talk to his master. As he was about to enter the master's room, he heard boisterous laughter. When he peeked through the crack in the wall, he saw that his master was busy entertaining guests.

Since it was starting to get dark, the disciples thought that they should light the lamps for the guests. But before they had time to light a candle, the master had cut a circle out of a piece of scrap paper and pasted it on the wall. Immediately, the circle turned into a full moon and the room became as bright as day.

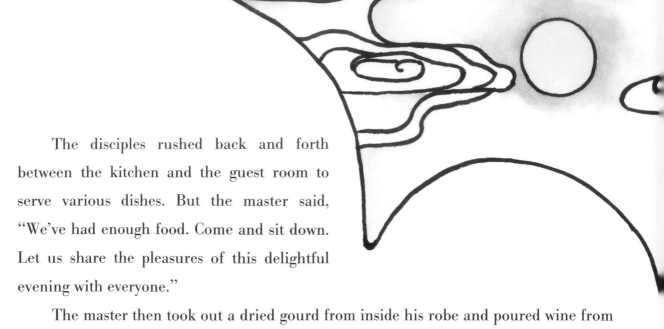

The disciples rushed back and forth between the kitchen and the guest room to serve various dishes. But the master said, "We've had enough food. Come and sit down. Let us share the pleasures of this delightful evening with everyone."

The master then took out a dried gourd from inside his robe and poured wine from it for his guests. Soon laughter filled the room and everyone started asking for refills. But Fei-long noticed that no matter how often the master served his guests, there was still more wine left in the gourd.

One of the guests emptied his cup in one gulp and said, "The moonlight is so dazzling, yet the beautiful fairy of the moon is all alone in her cold palace."

At this thought the guests wet their sleeves with tears. So the master picked up a chopstick and gently tossed it into the moon. In an instant, a slender young lady slid down the moonbeam.

"My burden is more than I can bear. Since I tasted my master's magic pear, I've been kept on the moon alone with nothing to do except to despair."

Her resonant voice brought tears to their eyes. And before anyone got a chance to say a goodbye, she floated up the moonbeam that turned back into a chopstick.

Drying his eyes on his sleeve, one of the guests cried, "Must we leave the lady of the moon all by herself in her cold palace? Why not share our last toasts with the lady in her pavilion?"

The master nodded and led the crowd slowly into the moon. And from where Fei-long stood, he could make out the drunken guests exchanging toasts while leaning against the pillars of the moon pavilion. After a while the moon began to dim until all that was left was a paper circle on the wall.

The next morning Fei-long went to his master and said, "As you predicted, the training here has been more than I can bear. The secrets of eternal life seem harder to grasp now than when I first met you. But before I leave, can you teach me just one small trick, so I can feel I have learned something?"

The master smiled and replied, "I can teach you anything you want, but without constant practice nothing can be accomplished."

"Master, I noticed that you always walk right through walls. I would like to learn this trick," insisted Fei-long.

"Very well," said the master. "Just whisper the phrase *tian kong wu xian jing* and walk through the wall."

Fei-long did as he was told but hesitated at the last moment, so the wall remained as hard as stone.

"Just rush through!" the master scolded him.

This time, Fei-long calmed himself and ran towards the wall with all his might. And when he turned around, he found that he was on the other side of the wall.

After thanking his master over and over again, he left the temple. When he arrived home, he boasted to his family that he had learned secret teachings from an immortal. But seeing that Fei-long hadn't changed much in appearance, nobody believed him. Finally when he became fed up with his family's lack of interest, he gathered many friends and relatives into the courtyard and shouted, "Today I will show you what I have learned from my immortal master at the Zhen mountains."

Then he recited the spell and ran towards the wall. But instead of disappearing through the bricks, he banged his head against the wall and fell unconscious. When Fei-long finally awoke he was surrounded by laughing faces, and could only sob in misery.

難字註解

immortal [ɪ`mɔrtḷ] *n.* 長生不老的人

p.2

banquet [`bæŋkwɪt] *n.* 宴會
plume [plum] *n.* 一縷（煙）

p.4

lacquered [lækəd] *adj.* 塗漆的
fearsome [`fɪrsəm] *adj.* 令人生畏的

p.6

stagger [`stægə] *v.* 蹣跚而行

p.9

monastery [`manəs‚tɛrɪ] *n.* 僧院；修道院
pester [`pɛstə] *v.* 煩擾，糾纏

p.10

treacherous [`trɛtʃərəs] *adj.* 變化莫測的

p.12

mischievous [`mɪstʃɪvəs] *adj.* 淘氣的
summon [`sʌmən] *v.* 鼓起（勇氣）
supervision [‚supə`vɪʒən] *v.* 監督，管理

p.14

disciple [dɪ`saɪpḷ] *n.* 門徒

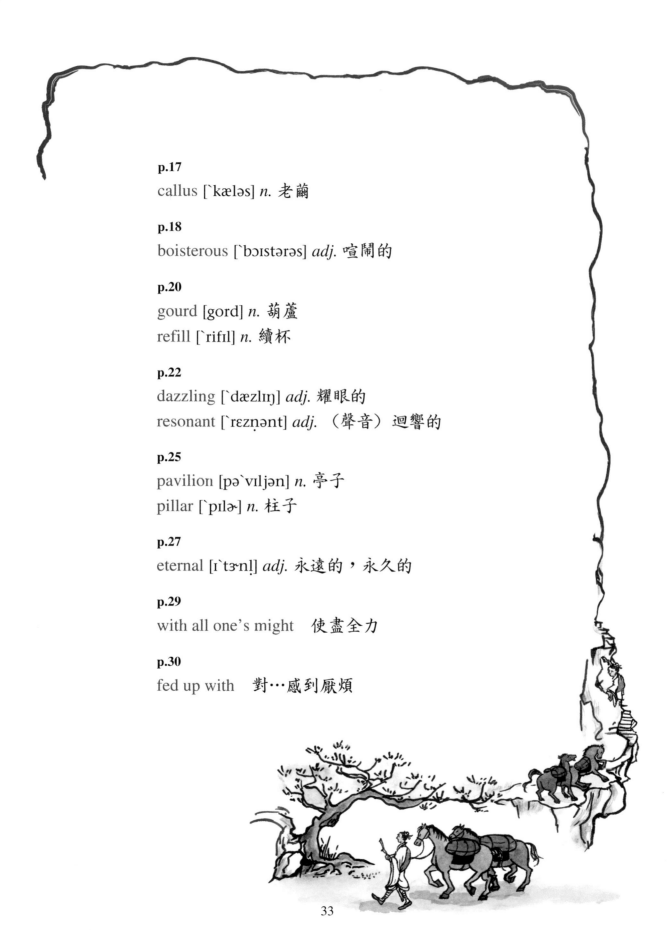

p.17

callus [`kæləs] *n.* 老繭

p.18

boisterous [`bɔɪstərəs] *adj.* 喧鬧的

p.20

gourd [gord] *n.* 葫蘆
refill [`rifɪl] *n.* 續杯

p.22

dazzling [`dæzlɪŋ] *adj.* 耀眼的
resonant [`rɛznənt] *adj.* （聲音）迴響的

p.25

pavilion [pə`vɪljən] *n.* 亭子
pillar [`pɪlɚ] *n.* 柱子

p.27

eternal [ɪ`tɝnḷ] *adj.* 永遠的，永久的

p.29

with all one's might　使盡全力

p.30

fed up with　對…感到厭煩

故事中譯

第二頁

　　在中國的京城，有一棟僕役成群的大宅子，裡面住著一戶豪門貴族。每年秋天，當糕餅舖開始烘焙月餅時，豪宅的主人都會設宴款待當地學者及官員們。今年，這位主人的兒子飛龍，頭一次被准許參加這個盛會。席間，飛龍從自己的座位看著這些貴客啜飲美酒，並觀賞著由煙斗飄升的陣陣煙霧。

第四頁

　　當滿月的月光悄悄的照入客廳時，賓客中一位最年長的學者用彩漆繪製的手杖輕敲大理石地板，吸引了大家的注意。他指著西邊輕聲說：「在我國邊境上有座高聳直入雲霄的山脈，其中的真山自開天闢地以來就是仙人的住所。我年輕時曾沿著蜿蜒的山路蹣跚而行，最後在一處令人生畏的懸崖邊，發現有座寺廟蓋在那兒。我從沒進去過那間寺廟，但聽說那裡的道士可以赤足在樹頂和山峰間跳躍而行，來去自如。」

第六頁

　　這些學者們在半醉半醒間仍啜飲著美酒，臉也變得和他們的絲袍一樣紅；唯獨飛龍聽得很專心，所以這位老者為他畫了張真山的地圖。

　　當所有賓客搖搖晃晃的起身感謝主人的招待時，大家已不知身在何處，也不記得席間的談話內容了。

第九頁

　　接下來的幾個星期，飛龍對真山念念不忘，他把地圖拿給他父親看，並哀求他允許自己出發到真山去。可是父親的回答一直都是「不准！」。

　　有一天，飛龍在父親上早朝時又拿這問題打擾他，令他怒聲大吼：「絕對不准！」他大聲咆哮著：「進真山裡的寺院？我這些年的光陰不是用來把兒子養大，讓他去當道士的！」不過，在飛龍一再央求之下，他最後還是只能祝福飛龍這趟真山之行。

第十頁

　　第二天，飛龍牽著兩匹背負他行李的馬出發了。經過數天的跋涉，山路變得險惡難行，最後飛龍不得不放棄所有的行李，包括那兩匹馬。正當他開始懷疑自己是不是被之前老者的話愚弄了的時候，飛龍發現了老者在地圖上所畫的山洞。於是飛龍點亮蠟燭，跪著爬進狹窄的山洞。當他接近窄道另一頭的亮光時，飛龍依稀看到一座懸崖上的小寺廟！

第十二頁

　　當飛龍抵達寺廟時，他看到一位鬍子又長又白的老人靜靜的坐在蓆子上。飛龍看不出這位奇人的年紀，因為他那狂野的眼神，使飛龍想起了在家鄉街道上遊蕩的野孩子。然而當老人以低沉的聲音詢問他的來意時，飛龍忽然覺得，再多的苦難自己似乎都能承受了。老人直視飛龍的雙眼，說道：「恐怕你會承受不了訓練。」

　　飛龍堅持著：「我保證無論如何都不會放棄的。」

　　「記住你說過的話。」這位老人說完，便隱身入寺院中。

第十四頁

　　隔天，中庭裡聚集了十名弟子，他們拿給飛龍一件粗質棉袍。飛龍換好衣服後，看到那些弟子們用手掬水，以手指刷牙，一滴水都不浪費。

第十五頁

　　接著，他分到一把斧頭，被派往山裡收集木柴。

　　當他帶著一大捆木柴回來時，又有另一份工作等著他：切菜。

　　晚餐過後，飛龍以為自己終於可以休息了，但他又被叫去劈柴好燒洗澡水。

第十七頁

接下來的幾個月，飛龍辛勤的工作著。他的雙手長滿了繭，身上的袍子也變得破爛不堪。飛龍每天都期望著工作能輕鬆點，但隨著冬天接近，白晝漸短，他的希望也跟著逐漸埋沒在雪中。不過既然其他弟子們毫無抱怨，飛龍也只好繼續每天收集木柴。

第十八頁

一個寒冷的冬日午後，飛龍再也無法忍受這種訓練了，他決定去找師父談談。正當飛龍要踏入師父的房間時，他聽到陣陣喧鬧的談笑聲。飛龍透過牆縫偷看，發現師父正忙著招待客人。

第十九頁

由於天色漸暗，弟子們想著應該為客人點燈照明。但就在他們點亮燭火前，師父已從一張廢紙上剪下一個圓貼到牆上，那張圓紙立刻變成一輪滿月，而整個房間也變得亮如白晝。

第二十頁

弟子們穿梭往返於廚房與客室之間，忙著端上各式菜餚。但師父開口說：「我們的食物夠多了。坐下吧，大家來共享這愉快的夜晚。」

接著，師父從衣袍裡拿出一個風乾葫蘆為客人們斟酒，整個房間很快就充滿了歡笑聲，大家也開始要求添酒。然而飛龍注意到，無論師父幫客人倒了多少次，葫蘆裡還是一直都有酒。

第二十二頁

一位客人將杯中的酒一飲而盡，然後說：「月光如此耀眼奪目，然而美麗的月中仙女卻得獨自一人守著她淒冷的宮殿！」

想到這裡，所有的客人都拿起了衣袖拭淚。於是師父拿起一根筷子，輕輕的丟進牆上的月亮裡。才一會兒功夫，一位身形纖瘦的年輕女子便隨著月光出現在眾人眼前。

「我的苦難實在令人難以忍受。自從吃了主人的仙梨後，我就一直被困在月宮裡，只能獨自悔恨。」

仙女的聲音迴盪在空中，讓每個人都濕了眼眶。在大家還來不及向她道別之前，仙女就已經飄盪在月光中，並變回了一根筷子。

第二十五頁

一位客人以衣袖擦乾淚水，喊道：「我們一定得讓月中仙女獨自一人，留在那淒涼的月宮中嗎？我們何不到她的亭中，與她一同分享最後一巡酒呢？」

師父點頭同意，並領著眾人慢慢進入月亮中。從飛龍站的地方看過去，他還能依稀看到那些喝醉的賓客，倚著月宮的亭柱互相舉杯的身影。過了一會兒，那個月亮開始變得朦朧昏暗，最後只剩下一張貼在牆上的圓紙片。

第二十七頁

　　隔天一早，飛龍告訴師父：「正如同師父所預言的，這裡的訓練非我所能承受。如今，永生的奧祕似乎比我初見您時更難領悟了。不過在我離開前，您可以教我一樣本領嗎？好讓我覺得自己有學到些東西。」

　　師父微笑著說：「我可以教你任何你想學的本事，但不持續勤加練習的話，是不會有所成就的。」

第二十九頁

　　飛龍堅持要求：「師父，我注意到您總是穿牆而過。我想學穿牆術。」

　　師父說：「那好，只要低聲念這口訣：*天空無限經*，並直接朝牆壁走過去即可。」

　　飛龍照師父的話做了，不過他在最後一刻猶豫了一下，所以牆依然像石頭一樣堅硬。

　　師父責備他：「直接衝過去！」

　　這一次，飛龍靜下心來，全力向牆壁衝了過去。當他一轉身，發現自己已經在牆的另一邊了！

第三十頁

　　再三拜謝過師父後，飛龍便離開了寺廟。他一回到家，便對家人吹噓自己已經向仙人習得了神祕的仙術。可是大家看飛龍的面貌並沒有多大改變，因而都不相信他說的話。最後，飛龍受夠了家人一副興趣缺缺的樣子，便邀集了許多親朋好友到庭院中，大聲宣佈：「今天，我要為大家表演在真山上，向我那神仙師父學得的仙術。」

　　接著他念出口訣，然後全速朝著牆壁衝了過去！然而，飛龍並沒有穿過磚塊到牆的另一邊去，反倒一頭撞上了那堵牆，昏了過去！等到飛龍醒過來時，周圍的人都在嘲笑他，而飛龍只能懊悔的啜泣著。

Exercise

separate	interrupt	make out
predict	accomplish	boast

Fill in the blanks with the words listed above. Make changes if necessary.

1. It's too dark for us to _____ who was coming towards us.
2. Nothing can be _____ without hard work.
3. The child was _____ from his family because of the war, and now he has become an orphan.
4. The boy _____ to his family that he is the fastest runner in his school.
5. Sorry about _____ you, but I have an emergency to report now.
6. The Central Weather Bureau (中央氣象局) _____ that this weekend will be raining a lot.

41

Reading Check

(A) The eight pictures below tell the story of *The Land of the Immortals.* Put number 1~8 under each picture in the correct order.

_____

_____

_____

_____

_____

_____

_____   _____

(B) Now, look at the pictures and try to tell the story in your own
   words.

Comprehension

1. What do you feel about Fei-long? What is his personality?
2. What do you think about Fei-long's immortal master? Why did he
   ask Fei-long to do things that are not related to what Fei-long
   wanted to learn?
3. Imagine you are Fei-long. Write a short passage to express your
   thoughts about your master.
4. What do you think will happen to Fei-long after he failed to walk
   through the wall?

Part 1

1. make out　　2. accomplished　　3. separated

4. boasted/boasts　　5. interrupting　　6. predicts/predicted

Part 2

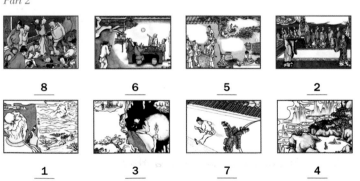

8　　6　　5　　2

1　　3　　7　　4

作者／繪者簡介

Machi Takagi and Jonathan Augustine have traveled throughout the world as husband and wife. They devote much of their time toward artistically expressing their fascination with cultural diversity. Machi Takagi is a painter of nihonga (traditional Japanese painting) and Jonathan Augustine is a professor of international communication at the Kyoto Institute of Technology in Japan.

作者Jonathan Augustine博士與繪者Machi Takagi女士夫婦的足跡遍佈世界各地。他們為文化的多樣性深深著迷，並藉著藝術形式記錄對各種文化的感情。Machi Takagi女士為「傳統日本畫」(nihonga)畫家，而Jonathan Augustine博士現為日本京都工藝纖維大學國際傳播教授。「仙人之谷」改編自中國《聊齋誌異》 中的短篇故事 「嶗山道士」，為Machi Takagi女士與Jonathan Augustine博士夫婦的共同創作。

愛閱雙語叢書

黛安的日記
Diane's Diary

Ronald Brown　著

呂亨英　　　譯

劉俊男　莊孝先　繪

中英雙語，附CD

想知道台灣女孩在美國生活，
會發生什麼事嗎？
看黛安的日記就知道了！

不得了了！在台灣土生土長的黛安，居然因為爸爸工作的關係，要跟全家人一起移民美國！日記就從放暑假的第一天開始，紀錄黛安一家人在美國生活、黛安參加夏令營等趣事。看黛安如何用輕鬆活潑的口吻，跟讀者分享她的新生活。

愛閱雙語叢書

給愛兒的二十封信
Letters to My Son

簡　宛 著

簡宛・石廷・Dr. Jane Vella 譯

杜曉西 繪

中英雙語，附CD

本書集結二十封作者給兒子的家書，作者以風趣流暢的筆觸，取代傳統說教方式，字裡行間盡是母親對兒子的關愛之情及殷殷期盼。這本溫馨且充滿母愛的中英對照書信集，為成千上萬的父母與青少年提供了最佳的溝通管道，也是最好的「悅讀」及學習英文的方式。

二十篇母子間的心靈對談
二十封溫馨感人的書信